Keep Running

Jane Carmody

Keep Running

Keep Running
ISBN 978 1 74027 877 5
Copyright © Jane Carmody 2014

First published 2014
Reprinted 2017

GINNINDERRA PRESS
PO Box 3461 Port Adelaide 5015
www.ginninderrapress.com.au

Contents

Shane

The challenging science of reading other people's minds didn't come easily to Shane. What Shane had taken as love, Sacha had meant as filling in time with an idiot. It was because she liked Derek, Shane's best friend, that she pursued the relationship. Derek, on the other hand, had the good sense to find Sacha repugnant. He did not condone the relationship that his mate had with her, although he said nothing, but felt her cloying presence excruciating.

Fourteen-year-olds possess little patience. The forbearance and perseverance Sacha needed to pursue Derek, while on the arm of Shane, tired her.

It was a day in early September when Shane had stood at the bus stop. He waited for Sacha. He watched as she walked nonchalantly down the street, clutching her mobile phone to her ear. He felt the sting of adolescent pleasure, anticipating the sweetness of passion that would take place on the unyielding timber seats in Lakeland Memorial Park.

'Look, Shano,' she said tucking her long black hair behind her ear and looking downwards, 'I can't go today. I can't… I'm not going out with you any more. So don't ring. OK? See you 'round.' She turned, raised the mobile back to her ear and walked away.

He stood as lean and cold and silent as the bus stop sign. He watched her disappearing form; her swaying indigo hips turn to jelly, morbidly detach at the waste and circle through a teardrop. He could not help but watch. The rise of tears to his eyes was both tragic and beautiful. He felt the intensity of pain, but his vision, made surreal by the tears froze him to the spot. The whorl of gunmetal, flesh and stretch denim, crystallising momentarily, before shattering onto the cruel pavement was an aesthetically fulfilling experience.

Derek found him at seven-thirty still standing on the corner, where three hours earlier Sacha had dumped him. The moon embalmed their forms with a gauze of white, and the street floated just above hell. Little by little, particles of road, rose and transmogrified into icing dust. Shane stared and tasted it.

'You're better off without her,' Derek said.

'What would you know?'

'I'm not arguing. I'm freezing my arse off, and your mum will wonder where you are. Let's go,' Derek said with authority.

It was not that Derek's year-and-a-half seniority made him wise; if anything, age differentials made people more crazy or take risks, or want to fight, especially around here anyway. Derek just acted his age. Many in this place did not – their minds got to a point of expansion and then they regressed. Some got to sixteen years of age before their minds went backwards; others were a little younger or older, before their minds became like the trees, stunted, blackened, starved. One person's thought became another's, not through careful consideration, but by lack of it. So when someone said that Shane was simple, it became a dictum that even his mother believed, but not truly.

This was Lake Melloway. And what a joke that name was. There wasn't any lake here most of the time – just a resentful crust of earth, blazed upon and burned – the softness gone out of it and its people. The town was dried out, any spill of hope evaporated.

'Where the hell have you been, you stupid little cretin? I've been worried sick,' Lorna's gravelly voice asked, when the boys entered the cream fibro house.

Shane ignored her and went straight to his room, slamming the door behind him. The red Lamborghini door poster fluttered and tore at the tape, creating a minor cyclone.

'They've broken up,' Derek explained.

'I told him, I told him,' Lorna lamented, raising her brow in an exasperated way then reaching for the last lonely cigarette in her pack.

'Yeah, I know.'

'Going to Melbourne, for the show, will take his mind off it. He's been mooning around for days over that girl, giving me the pip.' Lorna confided to Derek. 'Now, you take care of his money, Des. Oh, and the train ticket…you know…all the stuff. Thanks, Des. And for Christ's sake don't let him out of your sight. And don't let those other two, Wil and Kyle, stir him up or leave him stranded. Look, here's a tenner for your trouble.'

Derek honourably rejected the money at first, but he knew a tenner was a tenner and worth a quarter of his paper round. He also knew what it was worth to Lorna and so it became more valuable. She pressed the money into his hand.

Shane watched the transaction, sucking his lower lip as though he were a fool.

The potent diesel growled at low pitch, then rose to a more urgent note as it pulled out of the station. The boys took their seats in the empty carriage, and as they were the only occupants from the terminus they moved again and again. They pressed their faces against the window and saw the ever-diminishing figure of Lorna become a scribble on a bleached background. Shane stared, calculating how many times the figure of Lorna would fit into the frame of the window until the bold solid lines of the town silos stole window space.

By the time the train neared Melbourne, Shane's eyes were like camera lenses, snapping frames of life, his head filling with images upon images. This was the first time he had been to the city other than when Lorna and he went searching for the old man when he was little. He gave the bird to all the commuters standing on the city platforms as did the other boys when the haughty country diesel pounded through the stations, but he felt an awakening. Buildings, people, cars, graffiti, trees, variations of green as he had never seen at home. It was invigorating. He was being transported to a place of energy. It was to him a puzzle, with pieces flying.

As they drew into Flinders Street Station, Shane darted to the front of the train.

'Where are you going? We don't get off here. It's the stop after this one,' Derek explained.

'Need a leak.'

The next minute, Shane blew ugly kisses to the boys from outside the train on the platform. 'Stupid little prick,' he saw Derek mouth as he leapt from the seat. Paddling people away, Shane flew up the ramp. At the top he scanned the platform to see Derek launch himself just before the train slowly edged away. He took a run at the turnstiles and jumped clear, fleeing down Swanston Street, stopping, tasting, taunting like a gadfly.

He was giddy as he turned to see if Derek had made it past the lockjaw gate with the ten dollars in his pocket weighing him down. 'Ha,' he cried as he spied the khaki windcheater with 'sharp end' stamped across it. Shane took off again, up St Kilda Road, across the bridge as Derek gained on him. Shane knocked against people but gathered momentum as a comet gains speed from passing planets. Onward, onward he went, past the art centre, running, sprinting. He raced past the National Gallery moat, greedily sniffing the exhaust fumes tinctured with chlorine. Derek was just about within reach when Shane deviated, turned sharply right and ran through the gaping, grey granite arch, splattering himself on the window – the immense crying window of the National Gallery of Victoria.

Derek texted to Kyle, 'u keep goin. We r stuffd.'

The fact that a body – human remains from thousands of years ago – was lying in a box made Derek shiver. Shane could only see the repeated and reassuring pattern decorating it, the painted face, the black eyes staring out of time. He spun out of the room where the Egyptian art was held in a search of more.

Derek rubbed his aching neck and shoulders as he stared at the Great Hall's stained glass ceiling. Shane lay on the floor, squinting, the liquidness of colour pouring down on him. He quickly got up and was in another room where framed, haughty, peach-skinned men stared from ornate drawing rooms. The delicacy of lace, the sumptuousness of damask, the tenderest suggestion of creases on faces arrested Shane's attention as nothing ever had. He could not believe a person had painted it; had generated life through gentle manipulation of a brush.

Time slipped past like a soundless stream.

Through a doorway and into another room he saw it. He stood where another man had stood seconds earlier. The man appeared to be searching the painting, maybe to find a remnant of himself, and had walked off as though the painting were a lie.

But the painting was not a lie to Shane, it was a truth of such force that he could not move. The blackened eyes, grief-stricken, deformed with despair; he knew such truth. He wondered how the simple lines and colours could cry his tears. The woman's face, misshapen, unlike a normal face was weeping, feeling grief as enormous as any other human.

'Look, Des. See? See it?'

They could have been standing there an hour. Derek searched for his friend and tried to see. For his friend, he tried. But he lacked the clarity to extract the direct beam of genius and anguish that the picture projected. For the time being anyway.

Shane yelled, 'Someone's here,' as Derek knocked on the front door, shifting from foot to foot, crinkling the tenner in his pocket and noticing for the first time in his life the greenish colour of the brass bell.

'Can't you get it? You lump of...' Lorna said sharply as she opened the squeaking door mid-sentence.

'I'm sorry, Lorna, he just took off. Got out of the train. I thought he was going for a pee. Just ran into town and into that building. Where the green woman was – the weeping woman. I know he's been on and on about it. Here's your money back. I can't take it after losing him.'

'Don't talk to me about that weeping woman! Looks like she needs a facelift to me, Des,' Lorna said as she led Derek into Shane's room.

The marks of old crayons were scrawled, almost torn onto butcher's paper that rippled from the walls as they entered. Colour pulsed – crimson, magenta, yellow, ochre, green, sap green, acid green, emerald and lime green. Many weeping women hung from the walls, amongst other entities, who were born from Shane's mind. Derek saw the stack of art books – glossed and rich-looking – on Shane's desk.

'Yeah he even got me to go to the library, Des. He was desperate for the books. I don't know what's going to happen when we have to return them.'

The room silenced them briefly with its breathing walls. Shane was within somewhere observing them with incandescent outlines.

Lorna turned to Derek. She closed her hand over his as it held the precious tenner. 'You keep your money, Des. He wasn't lost. He was found.'

Specks and Gods

The slate-coloured Saab streaked past their XF Ford like it had been whipped by the devil. Flicking an arrogant spray from the rain soaked Tullamarine Freeway, it slid unctuously out of sight. Lana noticed the tightly coifed suited-up driver and with a thrill thought he might have been famous.

Their sluggish gold car had slimed its way through the wet inner city roads glued together with traffic. But now on the way to the airport they were going as fast as the car could. Lana knew better than to expect great speed so she sat tight in the passenger seat repeatedly staring at her ticket information – Qantas, six thirty-five – and secretly at the time on her mobile phone, given that the dashboard clock didn't work. Her fingers were working overtime tearing at the corners of paper.

Feeling her heart thwacking away at her chest, she blurted, 'I wish you were coming,' and looked straight ahead at the other traffic passing, receding from her vision and dissolving into the grey constant drizzle. She glanced across and regretted.

'Me too,' said Ian, her dad. She noticed the teary driver-side window and the paths of raindrops determinedly coursing across the buffeted surface. 'But who would look after Tess and Charlie if I came?'

Knowing that her younger sister Tess had been asked to stay at her friend Leah's house often enough and that the chubby baby Charlie could always find a home at Aunty Chris's, she felt sick at the thought. She ripped inside. Her mouth tightened with truth. She recalled earlier in the week clumsily snatching the 'Choir: Authority to Travel' letter to get her father's signature. It had been sitting on a pile of papers and the turbulence of air had caused the Newstart Allowance form to float dismally from the kitchen bench.

'April's mum is going. And Mrs Rocca will look after you.'

'I hate them,' Lara said, lashing straps of words at the closest thing.

She watched through the windscreen as wave after wave of rain pelted down, listening to the crazed tympanic drill upon the car and the foot-stomping whack of the windscreen wipers. Up ahead she saw the abrasive burst of stoplights and noted that it belonged to the Saab. At the traffic lights they pulled up behind it and once again they had to wait for their turn to go. Lana's fingernails scraped furiously at the paper.

Ian tapped the steering wheel and he leaned forward. 'It'll be OK, kid. We'll getcha there on time if this bloke in front moves 'is arse.'

As the light snapped green, the head of the traffic moved quickly through. The Saab remained stationary.

'Come on, you bloody idiot,' Ian barked as his busy hand searched for the horn.

After several seconds, the Saab skidded off leaving Lara and Ian to face the next round of red lights.

As soon as the Ford stopped next to the departure terminal, Lara jumped out and waited for Ian to open the boot. She pulled at the backpack and raced through the doors.

'Oh! Here you are.'

'Hello, Mrs Rocca,' Lara mumbled through ruddy lips.

'It's OK, pet. Plenty of time. Take your bags over there, Lara. Hello, Mr McLean.'

'Thought we'd be late,' he apologised.

'Yeees. Terrible weather. No matter,' Connie Rocca soothed as she lost eye contact and turned her head toward the girls.

'Just gotta move the car,' Ian explained as he retreated to the doorway.

'Sure. Sure, Mr McLean.'

Lara returned and sought her father in the rush of bodies. 'Mrs Rocca…?'

'Not now, Lara. I need to count.'

Lara strained to see the figure of her father amid the throng and watched as the other girls gave farewell kisses and hugs to their parents. Her head turned this way and that. She felt the pressure of holding a sob and her lips pursed.

'Come on, girls. We need to move now.' Mrs Rocca projected her stringy voice above the general din and, as she turned her head towards the gate, she almost grazed her neck on her starchy white shirt.

'Mrs Rocca, I can't see my dad.'

'He had to go, Lara.'

Through the door they went chirruping like birds, Lara hanging back and nearly unhinging her neck.

'Come on, Lara.'

She took one glance back and recognised the blue stretched woollen jumper dodging the moving masses. But by now she was in the line and was unable to go back. He blew a kiss. Mrs Rocca crinkled her mouth into a smile.

'Had to wait for that dopey Saab bloke on the crossing,' he yelled across the mob and broke into a familiar smile.

Lara smiled in embarrassment at the rogue grin. She kissed back and was swept up through the passage as though into a vacuum.

Lara's stomach felt too sudsy to care about the window seat and Marissa loved her for it. 'Do you want to listen to my iPod?' she gushed in return for a bumpy view of the terminal before it plunged into porridgy cloud. 'I love the window seat. Mum always lets me have the window seat when we go to the Gold Coast to visit Grandma. Wow. Here, have a look,' she waffled as she leant back into the cushion.

'It's OK,' Lara said.

'No, have a look.'

'Yeah, nice,' Lara complied.

She watched until the plane floated into the eerily wafting cloud. An intermittent orange glow reflected off the wingtip lights onto the softness. Like the southern lights. Aurora Australis. Aurora. The goddess of morning stepping her sugary pink slippers across the sky with Sol her brother in her wake ready to flaunt his showy coat tails. The early morning was heaping heavy images upon her drifting and sleepy head.

As they ascended to the troposphere above the segregating wall of clouds and into the realm of the gods, Sol blazed with such ferocity, she was momentarily blinded. The trolley trundled down the aisle with the promise of something exotic but in reality only overpriced, so she snoozed as Aurora padded across the sky, sprinkling rose-dewy drops. And through the wispy webs of dream reality she heard Marissa's iPod and the symbiotic crush-gush of air that raced around the plane, and the chatterbox girls surrounding her, and could smell the kick of coffee, and see her dad waving with his daggy knitted jumper.

And there he was waiting at the crossing while the man in the Saab sashayed across the crossing or a bridge of some sort, with his entourage, as though he were on a stage. He wore a garish crimson crushed velvet robe with rhinestones that he said were diamonds. But when someone interjected and said that the stones were green he answered that they were 'Ahhrgyle, Ahhrgyle,' and that seemed to placate everyone. Then he strode into the departure lounge and people fell about saying, 'There's a god.' One old grandma in a wheelchair rode up to him and touched his robe asking for a cure.

He turned with annoyance and then seeing her adoration, with all the benevolence he could muster (which wasn't much for a god) he told her to pick up her wheelchair and walk. Now that wasn't an easy thing to do – and she didn't do it, but all who heard him declare it said that it truly happened because other people had corroborated the story. And as the people crowded around the Saab man, the old grandma was overwhelmed by the swelling congregation and remained behind when the people followed the crimson robe, so her version didn't count.

And as the people left, only her father in his blue woollen jumper was there to pick up the wheelchair and the grandma and stumble away, falling many times, but they were happy in heart. The Saab man continued to walk or levitate to the departure lounge and his garments became radiant. He coughed and there were those who claimed that pearls came out of his mouth. And when they said that, others believed that they saw strands of phlegm as dainty beads. And some were scraping bits up off the floor with tissues, to be sold later when the value went up. He ascended the escalator and strode to the VIP lounge. But there he was met with a dilemma, for there were two entry doors. Of course the grand embossed door made of platinum was the obvious choice, for the other was draped with a heavy-duty plastic pest deterrent straps. Could it be a trap? Surely not. The other entrance must be for tradesmen and he definitely was not of that status. He felt the heavy gaze of the crowd upon him. He entered the platinum door. He was entitled.

'Wrong. Wrong,' thought Lara.

Zeus or Jesus or Buddha poked his head out from behind the strips and peered around. 'That was close,' he sweated, looking a little tired.

'…she's tired.

'Huh.'

'Rockie wants you to put your seat belt on for arrival. We're almost there.' Melissa said.

The bus was about fifty metres away waiting in the bright sunshine beyond the shade of the airport building. Mrs Rocca led the way. The girls walked in pairs along the stained path juggling backpacks or pulling compact little suitcases on wheels. Some of the girls were practising one of the songs they were to sing later.

'Oh, you sound like angels,' one elderly lady cooed.

Melissa and Lara trailed the girls but were blocked by three men in suits who had emerged from the terminal, their sprawling pinstripes expanding roundly out on to the footpath like giant fullstops. The girls stepped into the gutter to avoid them. Lara glanced briefly at the human obstacles when she brushed by. She smiled at the man that she had lightly touched and recognised the hair. She thought he looked at her, but he was inspecting a speck on his shoulder and brushed it off.

The Crossroad

'Damn the logbook,' George said, and Adam knew they were in trouble.

George drove into the car park as beachgoers skipped across the steaming asphalt. He jammed on the brakes and took three car spaces when he could have taken two, then he lit a cigarette.

Turquoise waves leapt at the bay beach. He exhaled languidly. The smoke was immediately swept away as though it had never been. He scowled and moved uncomfortably in the driver's seat resting his bronzed elbow on the window frame and held the cigarette as if it were precious.

'Hey, kid…' He was about to say something, but he left it hanging there, like a broken, but still attached, tree limb.

Adam didn't know what to do. It was twenty past five. The sun was too far down in the sky for comfort.

George's hazel eyes narrowed. He placed his grubbed Hardy Haulage cap on his head and said, 'Goin' for a little walk, kid.'

Adam glanced at the time on his mobile phone. 'Is he serious? Does he want me to come?' he thought.

George jumped out of the truck and walked purposefully to the boat ramp. Adam followed at a distance.

George stopped and studied a man who was easing his boat into the water and said. 'Goin' fishin', mate?'

'Yeah,' the man said distractedly as he wrestled with the trailer.

'What are you looking for? Snapper?'

'Yeah. Whatever comes my way. You do a bit of fishin'?'

'No, but I'm lookin' for a boat – wanta get into it.'

First time Adam had heard about that one, and he had heard many of George's plans after travelling around with him in the delivery van over the Christmas break. One day he started talking about taking up flying lessons when they had delivered some furniture in Moorabbin and saw a Cessna, nearly as big as the windscreen, breeze over Centre Road to land at the adjacent airport. Then he was going to take up golf after they went past Kingston Heath when the Australian Open was on. He even went to the pro shop and took a couple of clubs out on to the fairway to try out. Two shanks and three misses seriously tested his resolve, however he continued to talk about it for a week-and-a-half. But the fishing, that was new. Adam could picture him doing that – dropping a line in at the end of a pier and waiting for a bite. A good thing to do in retirement.

He stood and looked wistfully across the water, his heavy brow shading his eyes, as he scoured the horizon.

'What the hell is he looking for?' Adam wondered as he waited. Hoping. He knew that back at the yard the hulking figure of Mitch would be waiting, swearing, looking down the road then at his watch, ready to swing the gate shut on another day of drudgery with his usual angst and impatience. Eager to sink a tinny, shoot pool or find a wave. His face would start to redden with frustration. He'd flick back a dreadlock and wipe his besmirched face. He'd give the delivery truck a chance, maybe ten or fifteen minutes. But that would be it. Mitch wouldn't even try to contact them on the mobile, given that George had told them to 'Get stuffed' when the boss Neville organised for all the staff to have one a while back. George's phone was still in its box in the glovebox behind the screwed up pie wrappers and pens – like a relic. And they wouldn't phone Adam – probably didn't even have his number, and Adam wouldn't ring, couldn't ring. What would he say? George had lost it? Had gone senile? And only two weeks to go.

And that would be that. The truck would be locked out of the yard. George's car would be locked in. Adam would miss his lift with Aldo to the bus stop and would have to wait for another hour-and-a-half for the next one. But that didn't seem to be foremost in George's mind at the moment.

The heat mocked them in their protective drill overalls. Adam could feel its prickly touch needling him and the sweat steaming beneath his cap. Two glistening girls in bikinis walked past giggling, and Adam looked down.

'Mr Barnes,' he squeaked, 'it's nearly half-past.'

George continued to stare, beyond the horizon it seemed – to look into the imminent darkness past twilight. He looked dark as well, not just his navy clothing or his tanned arms. The shimmer of the sea, the bristling brilliance of the sky and the lively insolent intrusion of the sunbeams conspired to enforce the contrast. He blotted the landscape. He wasn't listening or he wasn't answering. Next to him the water slapped at the sea wall marking the endless battle between obsolescence and obstinacy.

It was an age before Adam spoke again. 'Mr Barnes, I think the gate will be shut.'

As though flesh had been cut, he reacted. He turned sharply. 'Why didn't you say so, youngster?'

'Was it my fault? Should I have spoken up?' Adam thought.

They walked back to the truck and sat for a moment in the scorching cabin. Then George stared into the distance again. Adam fingered the window winder waiting and watching for the turn of the ignition key. Here was George lost again in thought. The heat inside was exhausting.

Adam waited and wondered what would happen. 'Ya gonna take up fishing, Mr Barnes?' he said uneasily, trying to snap George out of his reverie.

'Yeah, thinkin' about it.'

The engine turned over, rumbling and shaking.

'Might take a look at that boat place on the way back.'

'But Mr Barnes, it's after five-thirty.'

'It's OK. If it's shut, I'll just look through the gate. I'll still see the boats,' he said with a simple smile.

'No, but I mean…'

'I know what ya mean, young fella.

The truck lurched as they rounded the corner unstably onto the highway. Cars packed around them as they neared the intersection with brakelights blazing like mortal messages. They had to wait for the traffic lights. George contemplated the direction he would take. The air conditioning spluttered like a smoker. Adam felt the vagaries of adult behaviour burdensome as they finally headed to Sail-Away Marine and Parts.

The salesman at Sail-Away was just closing the gate and yelling, 'Hey, you can't park there.'

But George wasn't listening and he got out of the truck blocking the driveway. 'What are them boats worth?'

'Mate, you'll have to come back tomorrow. No one can help you now.' The salesman sweated through oily skin, wet around the armpits, smoothing his shining hair.

'Mate,' George stressed, 'I may not be here tomorrow.'

Adam watched and listened as George wrote down prices. He looked almost convincing. But the boat salesman flicked the sweat from his brow and hurried off.

'You could live on one of them boats,' George explained as he gazed at the price list through his scratched glasses. 'That would be pleasant…I s'pose.'

'Yeah. My mum's uncle bought one to live on in Queensland when he retired.'

'Did he now? Did he fish?'

'Yeah, I think so. I don't remember very well. He didn't have it very long…had a heart attack and died not long after he bought it.'

'Shit!' George hurriedly folded the price list and shoved it into his back pocket.

The cab rumbled as the engine roared into life again and George continued the conversation. 'What, did he have heart problems before that?'

'I dunno, I was about six when it happened. We didn't see him a lot.'

'What did he do for a livin'?'

'I think he drove one of those really big trucks in the mines.'

'He drove a truck?' George scowled heavily as a new-model car cut in front of him.

'Yeah. But he did other stuff too. I think he worked at Gladstone in the aluminium place for a while, an' another factory that made car parts.'

'Car parts? Mmm,' George took a self-satisfied breath, as he shifted up from one gear to the next ever so smoothly – but a little roughly down again to the low gears as the traffic slowed.

'An' what are you gonna do with your life, youngster?' George asked, looking into his rear-view mirrors to find the road diminishing diametrically and shakily.

'I dunno. I can't leave school yet. Mum wants me to stay until year twelve but Dad says I should do a trade. I reckon it'd be good to be a mechanic, but I really like doin' graphic art too, an' music, you know, that sort of stuff. I like sport too.'

Adam blushed as he blurted and then retreated to his normal default position of adolescent reticence as though he had revealed too much of the rich network of roads he could choose to take. And George stopped talking. The road he was taking was demanding his attention.

Adam could still feel the sun belting onto his fair skin through the window of the cab even though cool air was being blasted through the vents. He gazed out the window at the passing suburban houses – some newly painted, some dilapidated and some removed altogether and replaced with other houses in brazen new styles. Then he returned his gaze to the traffic and snatched a glance of George with his weathered hands gripping the steering wheel, holding on for dear life and the concentration on his face ever aware of changes in the traffic.

'Do you think you'll get a boat, Mr Barnes?'

'Awh, I'll do the numbers. Maybe I'll have to stay at work a bit longer to afford it,' George said unexpectedly.

'Really?' Adam coughed, anxiously remembering the stored cartons of beer and mixed drinks for the much anticipated farewell party. 'Will you tell the boss?' he asked, confused.

'Ha ha, of course I'll have to tell the boss.'

'What a strange thing to do,' Adam thought, unbalanced by the crooked knock of human unpredictability and frailty. He then started to recognise the roads – his own neighbourhood roads. The truck jolted past the local bus stop where Adam's bus would be stopping soon. He wasn't sure if George was taking him home or if this was another detour. A few metres past the bus stop George pulled over and looked across to the road where Adam lived. The unmade road ascended scenically, winding through blooming bush and lofty trees.

'I can't get up there. I'll have to leave you here. Is that OK? I need to go a different way.' He added, winking, 'Not quite sure which way yet.'

'Yeah, yeah, thanks, Mr Barnes.'

Adam tossed his backpack on and jumped from the truck gleefully realising that he would arrive home earlier than if he had taken the bus. He ran across the road and turned to wave, but George was already shifting gear and pulling out from the kerb. Adam thought for a moment and in his naivety considered that he should have offered George some directions back to the depot. Then he thought a little more and realised that George probably knew more than he did. He stood at the corner and watched as the truck rumbled up the street. The laboured, tired grind of gears could be heard rising to a crescendo. Then he heard the brakes, as the truck came to a halt at the crossroad.

Golden Girl

Blonde hair reflecting the sun, it could have been gold filigree or even wire. Green eyes stared at me for a moment and then looked away. I hated her.

It was a punishing summer. The world was heating up; there had been no rain for weeks. There was brutality in the weather and it made everything brittle. The insubstantial clouds floated by in tantalising drifts. Our house was cloistered, isolated from the bleached bones of summer. The interior walls were painted with shades of sea mist, pine forest and mint. The carpet softly reflected the spill of moonlight on a cool night. A constant temperature of twenty-three degrees existed in most rooms and the curtains were always drawn against the sun. If I had not left the house during the hot months, I would not have been able to imagine that the heat outside was as suffocating as the air inside.

My mother chose to stay indoors for most of summer. Never a fan, of course, dry days. It was not good for her complexion or constitution, she said. Her trips to and from work were in an air-conditioned car. Atomisers filled with rose water accompanied her on her trips and where possible she was flanked by my father who lavished cool drinks and ample shade upon her.

She had no understanding of the relentless sun that I endured when I walked to and from the station to board the train for uni. The poverty of trees and grass in our new estate gave rise to dust storms and the flight of acid clay particles that coated my skin. I reached home before her most days and had time to cool down and freshen up before she saw me so she had no idea of the grime that attached itself to my sweat. On the days that I reached home after her, I was so conscious of my ravaged appearance that I avoided her and went straight into my room from the rear of the house through a back sunroom. I would groom myself before I appeared before her, studying my image in the hall mirror. Even then she would comment that I needed to wash my hair or put cool water on my ruddy face, or worse still have a shower which would obliterate any part of the outside world or maybe even me.

In the evenings she would venture outside when the sky had turned the colour of deadly nightshade. Dad would join her if he were at home. They would sit by the pool with a glass of red wine and talk – Dad choosing well-oiled words that would slip easily into my mother's ears. I could hear their conversations, as the pool was just outside my bedroom and the window open. I chose to keep the window open and the cooling vent off as I couldn't bear the artificial air or the waste of energy.

One stifling night, as the heat closed in on me, I tossed in my bed in an attempt to find a cool spot. The hours strung on and on like beads on an ugly necklace. I lay in my bed and felt the slippery droplets of perspiration form and trickle onto the sheet. I opened my eyes and my attention was caught by the albumen streaks shed by the pool lights upon the shantung curtains. I felt the irritation rise as the light seemed to grow and spread into the room. The annoyance was magnified by the effort to ignore it. Why don't they turn those lights off? They're sitting there oblivious to my need for sleep, drinking their stupid wine. My anger was building and coiling in a way that you have no control over. My stomach started tightening and squeezed minuscule sacks of air out of my lungs so that my breathing became shallow. My jaw set and my teeth ached from tension.

I felt myself sit upright, throw my legs out the side of the bed, rub my face roughly and stamp to the window and open it wider. By the time I had reached the window, the unfamiliar anger had subsided slightly, and upon the shock of eye contact with my mother, it had almost diminished.

'When are you going to bed?' I asked with the intensity of each word lessening.

'Darling, are you still awake?' she asked, as though she had been startled by my existence. 'Why don't you have a swim to cool you down? I never see you in the pool these days. Or open that duct in your room to let some nice cool air in,' adding, 'you crazy girl,' to savage any pleasantness I may have interpreted.

'No!' I snapped. The ashes of anger glowing red. 'How long will you be?'

'I don't know,' she said, languidly examining the glowing bulb of red wine in her hand. 'Perhaps all night.' She faced me and I could see the flash of light across her white perfect teeth.

'But it's annoying. The light is so bright in here.'

'Well, you're not helping yourself, Lauren, cooped up in that hot room. Just open the vent. The cooler is on. Or have a swim. You never use the pool.' She chewed on the wineglass and turned her head away towards my father, who raised his eyebrow from above the security of the business pages of the newspaper.

'It's not the heat, it's the light.'

She turned to me with the edges of her mouth conjuring a smile 'Of course it's the heat.' Again she peered at the glass she held. 'Stupid bug,' she spat as she dipped her crimson polished nail in to gouge a struggling gnat. She pressed it onto the bricks – the life gone out of it.

I sensed my eyes beading from wormlike frustration. I felt black and invisible in the cave of my bedroom.

'You are so difficult lately,' she breathed in a controlled way.

There was no answer except attack or retreat. My energy was draining too much for attack. For now, the windows slamming shut ensured safe defence.

'Just turn the light out and go to bed,' I called in terror before it shut.

She laughed in a mirthless way. 'That's funny, you telling us what to do and we're the parents.' And then as if dealing with another gnat, she said furiously, 'I don't know what is wrong with you.' Then she said to Dad, 'See, that's what I mean, Ed,' loud enough for me to hear, like a missile fired overhead as a warning. I knew she was looking at my window, and although it was an opening to the darkness of my room it only reflected the brilliant light where she sat.

It was six-thirty a.m. and I took wooden steps to the kitchen behind my folio of illustrations.

'So you finally got to sleep,' she startled me with – not so much a question as a statement – above the pale toast she offered.

Of course I did. Everyone does at some point during those restless nights, but that doesn't mean that they have rested peacefully or are refreshed. My eyes were stinging with lack of sleep and the world around me buzzed a little like a radio station not quite tuned in. I could feel her staring at me as I struggled with my folio and sat at the table.

'Busy day today?' she said, not waiting for an answer. 'I'll probably be home late today. We have a meeting. I've arranged for Dad and me to have dinner after. Can you feed the cat? There's a meal for you in the freezer to zap. Make sure you eat it this time. Haven't you eaten that toast I cooked yet? God, look at the time.'

I opened the container of orange juice and lifted it to my mouth to drink out of. She snatched it from me, causing some of the contents to spill down my top.

'What the hell…'

'Drink it properly. In a glass.' She picked one up and held it close to my face.

I could see the red capillaries in her eyes through the matted barbs of mascara.

'Why can't you do things the right way.'

I picked up the folio and banged past the table.

'Finish your breakfast, Lauren.'

I snatched up my bag and brushed past her white cold figure, up the passage and out into the boisterous day.

'Come back here and eat,' she howled to the wind.

I walked up the street baring the juice stain as though it were a war wound, and wrestled with my folio against the rising northerly. I could feel the heat beginning to bear down and sap the life out of the earth —the shadows growing smaller providing fewer places to shelter. I was exhausted before the day had begun.

As I was walking home from the station, I could feel the moisture forming on my upper lip and tasted the salt drying on it. The northerly was pounding away blustery and shouting in its usual way, trying to bully me backwards. It was difficult to push against it especially carrying my folio, which acted like a sail and got caught in the gusts. But I felt a stringy strength to get home to the haven of my room where I knew the battering would cease, where I could relax. For a while anyway.

The room gave me some relief, even though it was hot. I peered through the curtains and saw the pool lagoon-like, the surface fluttering, nestled by the lush ferns and small exotic trees. In a moment I was in, floating, facing upward – the sun splashing heat on my face, and the rest of my body shrinking under the surface. I kicked with short, sharp flicks and floated into the soft shadows. Drafts of jasmine breeze swept across me. The tendrils of the ferns made ballet movements, dipping and leaping tremulously. The drooping canopy of leaves flickered across the vault of sky.

And then a cloud appeared.

I thought that I heard movement in the house. I could hear doors being opened and shut. I feared.

The back door opened and my mother appeared. 'You scared me. I didn't hear you come in.'

'Well, you scared me. I thought you were staying back at work,' I said as I ascended the steps of the pool, revealing frail skin.

'My God, look at you,' she said, as knives of sunlight speared me and the wind knocked against the jittery goose flesh. I wanted to protect myself against the onslaught of the elements and searched for the towel. But it was behind her. I was subjected to the ferocity.

'What is happening to you?' she screeched. 'You're skin and bone…'

The winds swirled and curled around her gnarled words as I rushed at the back door. I fled to my room past the hall mirror and I glimpsed her – the blonde hair, coarse and lank, framing an ugly stretched face with bulbous green eyes. I hated her.

The Light

The sun lit the southern end of the porch with a buttery light. Spreading thinly, it dripped along the guttering, slipped along the rusty downpipe and spilt out into a pale pool around Ed's feet. He moved his chair and his body was dipped in light again away from the shadows. He tilted his head back and felt the strained warmth upon his face. Taking his left arm with his right hand, he caressed and rubbed it. Through the flannelette shirt and the bandages his arm throbbed. It felt foreign and swollen and useless.

He squinted and noticed the magpies on the tree, like burnt offerings on a stick against the sun, and gum leaves shivering around them. He hoped they would sing. But the afternoon was too still, sacredly silent, like the earth had stopped rotating for one golden moment. An image conceived in trickery to make you think that nothing would ever change again. The air was still wintry warm but it would cool quickly when the sun disappeared and its deft icy fingers would pick at his bones.

Ed picked up the newspaper. He started to read and then he re-read the shapes of letters jamming them into his head, but his head was full and not responding. So he turned to the sports section and scanned the miserable countenance of the Australian cricket captain who had made a duck in England. There was a profile of Roger Federer and he wondered how much insight you could gather from someone who always won.

The phone rang. He listened to his recorded greeting with displeasure. 'Sound like a bloody old fool,' he told Reggie the border collie, as he listened again to his daughter's voice on the new contraption she had rigged up and was now benefiting from.

'Hi, Dad, it's Glenda. I'll pick you up at ten tomorrow. See you then. Bye.' The rehearsed message brisk enough to avoid the risk of conversation.

'Such busy lives,' he lamented to Reggie, who lay as flat as a snake next to him. But he would have to engage his daughter in conversation some time later that night to tell her that the appointment had been cancelled and make up some reason why.

The expanse of sunlight started to creep away. First of all it receded from the western edges, backing away from the shadows of the sullen gums and then up onto the bleached weatherboards reflecting back with diminished strength. Ed felt the coolness in his feet. The blue air gathered and moistened around his tartan slippers, then ever so slightly it crept up the threadbare cotton drill of his work trousers until he was consumed by the dampening winter shade.

'Better take all this inside,' he explained to Reggie, as he started to gather the pipe, the tea-stained mug and the papers. But he didn't move off the chair, instead savouring the transition from afternoon to evening. One magpie burst through the silence like a cantor in a holy ceremony. And then the next chimed in, and the next, and next – their melodies clashing but harmonic, creating strings of minor notes that rose and twisted like a musical helix.

He knew that they would grow tired of their songs and fly hawk-winged to the porch railing, whacking the air with turbulent fury. They would wait impatiently, complaining like indulged children for their treats. Tonight it would be pieces of lamb left over from tea two nights ago when Glenda, her toddler and little girl had visited.

The phone rang again and Ed scooped up the papers, pipe and cup and listened. He could hear Ella saying, 'Hello. Hello, Grandpa…'

'Hold your horses,' he said to the phone as he hurried to pick it up.

'Hi, Grandpa,' said Ella. 'Where were you?'

'On the porch, honey. Where were you?'

'Here, Grandpa. Where else would I be?' she giggled. 'Grandpa, Mummy says that for tomorrow you have to bring the X-rays and the…what else, Mummy?…the doctor's letter.'

'Elly-belly, tell Mummy, when you hang up, that I don't have to go tomorrow. But don't tell her yet or I'll get into trouble. Can you do that?'

'Yep. OK. How's Reggie today? Did he play with the ball? I wish I could have a dog. My friend Lucy got a dog. A black one. A bit like Reggie an' he's a pup an' he widdled on the carpet…' she said, giggling again.

'Yeah, well, Reggie never did that. When your Grandma was alive, she wouldn't ever let him inside. When we first brought him home and he stayed in the shed an' oh did he cry.'

'If I had a dog, I'd sneak him into bed with me,' Ella whispered. 'Don't tell Mum. Are you gonna come and stay with us? Mummy said you might because you're sick.'

'Did she now?' Ed said with emphasis, 'Tell Mum I'm fine.' The force of the words shocked him and he felt ashamed. His voice mellowed and warmed. 'I'm not sick, Ell. Listen, maybe you can come and stay here. And don't tell Mum but you can have the dog in the house to pat.'

'Oh, can I? Can I have him in bed with me?' she said quietly.

'Well, I don't think Reggie would want to do that. He's a kind of a restless dog at night – a bit like me. But he might stay in the room with you for a while, maybe until you fall sleep.'

'And what about the magpies – have you fed them yet?'

'No, but they're out there squawking and pestering me for the scraps you didn't eat the other night, you naughty girl.'

'Well, it's just as well I didn't eat them, hey, Grandpa? Now the birds have got something to eat.'

'Oh, you're a smartie, aren't you?'

'Yes, I am.'

'And how's Heidi, my other smartie?'

'She's good, but she keeps losing my dolls.'

'They might need a place to live.'

'Yes, that would be a good idea. Grandpa, I've got to go and have my tea now. Love ya. See ya. Oh, I think Mummy wants to talk to you. Bye.'

'Oh God, no,' Ed muttered to himself. 'Bye.' It was reflex – the way he pressed his index finger down on the receiver.

He walked to the kitchen, opened the fridge and searched for the meat for the birds. Shifting an opened block of cheese he noticed the hardened yellowing edges and replaced it on the shelf. On the lowest shelf he moved the plate containing two remaining pieces of apple pie that Glenda had bought from the supermarket for sweets. With his gaze lingering on the pie, he picked it up and shoved a mouthful in. He finished it in three bites, saving the crust for Reggie, who had followed him into the kitchen and stood studying Ed wistfully. 'There you go, not too much or you'll get fat like me,' he told him, rubbing his stomach.

Behind the plate he found the leftover lamb and took it to the table, where he cut up the pieces for the birds.

The phone rang and Glenda's voice rang out. 'Dad, it's Glenda. What's happening tomorrow? If the doctor's changed the appointment time, could you let me know when it is…I'll have to organise work. Did the nurse come to change the dressing? Oh, and make sure you have the doctor's referral with you for the visit to the oncologist… OK…I'll see you soon…'

'Yes, sirree,' he answered from afar as he placed the morsels on the plate and then walked through the squeaking wire door to the porch, Reggie following expectantly. The birds had gone., the evening being too advanced for them to stay. He looked out onto the inkblot horizon, the gum trees solemn and yielding a faint aroma, but he was troubled by the insistent blaze of newly installed streetlight.

'Damn houses,' he complained to Reggie, who in turn looked up with mournful eyes as though recounting his days chasing Friesians. 'Come on, dinner time.'

Reggie abruptly stood wagging his tail. Before Ed went inside, he threw an impatient glance at the needling light that struck through the trees. 'Next thing they'll make me cut those trees down.'

The door creaked shut as he and the dog went inside for the night.

Jolene came around to the side porch at eleven-thirty in the morning. She found Ed carving a miniature chair for Ella's yet to be completed dolls' house. Reggie was lying faithfully at his feet eyeing a steaming mug.

'Hello, I thought I'd find you around here.'

'Hello, nursey. How are you? You're in good time. I've just made some tea. Want a cuppa?' he said, rising to go inside.

'Yep. I've been flat out. How's that arm of yours?'

'Yeah, good.'

'Was the doctor happy with it?'

'Ah…I wasn't able to go.'

'Oh,' Jolene said with concern. 'Well, that's a bit naughty.'

Indignant at being chastened, he didn't answer, but thought, bugger her and all those people telling me what to do.

'Yeah, well, I'm a naughty bloke,' he replied, placing the tea roughly on the kitchen table.

'This is the second time,' she said, her voice rising and falling just at the end to soften the pitch.

'Look, I'm an old bloke. They're better off spending their resources on youngsters.'

'Oh, OK. I'll let 'em know at the clinic to take Mr Field off the list…leave him to his own devices. Maybe that dog can lick your wounds,' she said, half smiling.

'That dog happens to be very intelligent – like its owner,' he explained, grabbing the biscuit tin.

'Well, the old dog isn't showing much intelligence at the moment.'

'OK, maybe I'm not that intelligent, but at least I can bake,' he said as he thumped the tin on the table. She peered in to find some chocolate royals.

'Mmm, delicious. You must give me the recipe,' she replied as she bit into the biscuit.

'I couldn't possibly. It's a family secret,' he said gruffly.

'I might ask your daughter then.'

'Oh, God no. Don't get her involved.'

'Really? Why not?'

'She doesn't bake and she doesn't talk, she just works. No, the secret dies with me.'

'That's not fair to the world.'

Ed filled the kettle again – the domestic rite that insisted on company. 'You'll have another?'

'No, no, I'll be widdling all the way back to the clinic. Is that what you want?'

'Get it in ter ya. It's not my fault if you can't control your bladder. You should get some of those undies the old girls have. There must be plenty in stock.'

'Ha,' Jolene laughed, accepting the tea feebly.

'In fact, bring some for me next time. I could wear them all day and not have to get up at all.'

'Oh, I thought that you didn't want us nurses back.'

'I know you'll be back. I'm irresistible.'

'Really?' Jolene said dramatically. 'Well, what about that dog and the birds you feed? You'll have to get up to do that.'

'They only get fed at night.'

'Well, what about when your daughter and grandkids come around? You'll have to get up then.'

'Nup. They only get fed at night. At least, I think so, and they usually bring the grub.'

'So, what will you do all day, sitting there in your wet nappies?'

'Stare and dribble,' Ed said defiantly.

'That doesn't sound like you, Mr Field. You'd get bored in the first ten minutes.'

'Maybe I would, maybe I wouldn't. I'd like to try it and see.'

'Are you going to need them before or after you finish that dolls' house and that furniture?'

'Dunno,' Ed said, looking at the carefully crafted pieces he had already made and the timber for the rest. 'Why do you nurses come around and upset blokes?'

'That's our job,' she said as she rinsed the mug and stood it on the sink. She arranged her bag on the table, 'Come on, let's get this over with. I've never had such a difficult patient.' Jolene carefully took Ed's arm and placed it on the table, unwrapped the bandages, which were hardened with congealed blood. 'It's healing well,' she said, disposing of the old bandages and taking out a new roll. 'You need to see that oncologist, Ed,' she said ever so softly but with a metal undertone that barred lightheartedness.

Ed shifted on the hardwood kitchen chair. He locked his eyes on the dog that stared back hopefully. 'What if I can't be bothered?' he asked eventually.

Jolene didn't smile. She packed each thing deliberately and silently into her satchel. 'You need to discuss all of the alternatives with your doctor. This can be managed.'

'You medical types, you think you have all the answers,' he said more angrily than he meant.

Jolene placed the satchel on the floor as the dog sniffed it. 'No, not all the answers, but we can ease the situation, we can help. You need to accept some help, Ed.' She picked up the satchel and turned to him. 'Any help can be arranged – for around the house, if you want to go out with some other folk, if you're feeling a bit low.'

'Low, be buggered. I'm bloody well OK. Me an' me dog, we're all right.'

'Look, I'm just saying…OK, I'm off now. Don't get up. I'll see myself out.'

Ed stood abruptly to show her to the front door. 'I will get up. You might pinch something on the way out.'

'Yep, well, that's why I carry this bag.'

'I thought it was to hit patients with.'

'Now, that's a good idea. If you don't watch out, you may be the first,' Jolene said as she noticed the vivid flourishes of the leadlight window, before stepping outside.

'No, not me, nursey. I'm too fast for you.'

'Might see you tomorrow,' Jolene said through the driver's window.

The car bumped along the driveway as the dappled sunlight slid along the shiny duco.

Ed noticed the green mass of grass in the paddock and after discussing it with Reggie thought he would buy a cow.

Ed was restless in the waiting room. 'I'll take the girls for a walk to the cafeteria,' he told Glenda.

'No, Dad, you'll be next. Stay here.'

Ella sat close to Ed and whispered, 'What's the surprise, Grandpa, at your place? Can Reggie stay inside tonight with us?'

'Reggie can stay inside,' he whispered, 'but there's another surprise and you'll have to wait.'

They returned to the house in the afternoon. The low sunlight radiated the porch as Reggie excitedly followed Ella and Heidi.

'You shouldn't be taking Ella for the night. I think it's too much for you,' Glenda said as they stood on the porch watching the girls install their dolls into the rooms of the dolls' house. 'Why don't you come and stay with us?'

'Maybe,' Ed said as the magpies chortled and flashed their wings.

'Why won't the magpies come down from the trees?' Ella said distractedly.

With more knowledge than he was ready to acknowledge, Ed said, 'It's not time for them yet.'

The Night of Sprinkle Stars

It was the night of sprinkle stars that Evie opened her eyes and began to see.

*

The family had stood at the back step of their brick-veneer home, as the radiant heat sweated off the house. Above them, in the deep indigo, a profusion of twinkling lights trailed across the sky.

Amy said it was a meteor that had disintegrated when it came through the earth's atmosphere.

Paul, the father, watched through a cigarette haze further away.

Marie, the mum, said, 'You know, this is a good omen.'

'You're so gay,' Amy snapped. 'It's a natural occurrence. You're always on about omens and prayers and meanings. Get over it. It's just a meteor shower.'

'No, it's an omen, you'll see,' Marie persisted, stirring the warm air.

Amy looked at her mother. The cheekbones, tip of her nose and upper lip caught the light from the sky, making her glow. Her eyes flickered with reflected starlight. The look of wonder made Amy wince. 'Mum, look at you. You're like a kid,' she said, hoping to hurt.

'Yes,' she said, 'isn't it great.' And she smiled with teeth agleam.

A mosquito squealed against the bug zapper.

Amy turned her back and stepped inside the breathless house. The noise of television was pounding against the close walls. The lights blazed. She walked doggedly up the hall toward her room. 'You still awake?' she asked Evie, her sister, whose bedroom was opposite hers.

'Yeah…just finishing some stuff for uni. What's going on? I heard you all sound excited about something.'

'Falling stars.'

'Falling stars? What? Like *Dancing With the Stars?*'

Amy burst out laughing. 'No, idiot. A meteor shower.'

'Sounds interesting,' said Evie distractedly, still tapping at her computer.

'It's pretty.'

Evie stopped typing. 'What's it like?'

'Well, you remember stars?'

'Real stars?'

'Yes, real stars, as apposed to shit stars on TV. Well, there's a sky full of them. It's unreal.'

'I thought you said they were real.'

They laughed.

'Real, unreal, surreal, it's all of those. It's pretty amazing. I've never seen anything like it before.'

'I wish I could see that.'

At once Amy felt burdened by her sight and said, 'Yeah, well, it's not that great. I mean, we can't see it that well.'

Evie, aware of the guilt she inflicted, couldn't help a sigh. 'You were out there forever. It must be pretty special.'

'Well, it's unusual, that's all,' Amy said, regretting her description, and felt a need to attack something. 'Mum says it's an omen.'

And both girls laughed again.

Amy wiped the perspiration from her upper lip. 'I'm going to bed. I'm stuffed. Night, No Eyes.'

'Night, Four Eyes.'

Amy moved the curtains back and peered out into the night from her bedroom window. The light show had finished and in the absence of the fleeting brilliance, the more subdued stars that had been obliterated, took their place and blazed again. Amy stared into the sprinkled light against the darkness and wondered for a moment. She knew that nebulas were out there and new stars and black holes were being formed too. She knew that at some point in the distant heavens, time and light were skewed. But she couldn't see it. Was that faith? No. It was science. That's what she believed. She recalled the childishness of her mother and felt embarrassed for her.

Amy climbed into bed and reached for her book. The words looked black and greedy. She tried to read once and then again. By the third time, she took her glasses off, dropped the book by her bed, pushed back the sheet and turned out the light. Her lids were heavy. She opened them to make sure that Evie's light was out and fell into a deep sleep.

It was three o'clock in the morning. The house had cooled from a change that had come through in the night. The cream light from Evie's lamp lit Amy's wall, creating not quite light, but darklessness.

'Amy, are you awake?' Evie whispered at Amy's bedside.

The blunt blows of consciousness pounded through phases of sleep. Amy woke through the turbulent passage. 'What? What's the matter? Are you OK?' she asked, her eyes wide and wild.

'Ame, Ame. I can see.'

Hard bursts of reality came down heavily on Amy. Evie must have been dreaming. She must be sleepwalking. Amy damned herself for telling Evie about the stars. She hated herself, and therefore she hated Evie.

'Go to bed.' She tossed her feet to the floor and felt the coldness. As she sat up, she looked at Evie, who was following her with her eyes. 'Come on,' she said with grits of anger. 'You're freaking me out.' She enclosed Evie with her arms. 'Let's go.'

'I can do it,' Evie said calmly.

Amy put her arms around her sister and directed her to the door.

'You don't understand, Amy. I can do it,' Evie said. She detached Amy's arms, and looked straight into her eyes.

'Look, don't shit me. Let's go. I just want to go back to bed.' The layers of sleepiness were being peeled back, and Amy was starting to question. She had never had to deal with a sleepwalker before and she wanted to know. 'OK, you do it. I'll stay here.' Amy lied for she knew she would have to follow.

'Night, Amy,' said Evie as she turned for her room.

Amy tiptoed to the door to follow.

Evie turned to face Amy. 'I thought you weren't going to follow me.'

'Geez, you've got good ears,' Amy said. 'OK, get into bed then.' She entered Evie's room and watched as she covered herself with the blanket.

Instead of feeling for the light switch, Evie turned to the lamp and pressed it. 'Night, Doubting Thomas.'

'Yeah. Night, No Eyes.'

Amy returned to her room, unable to see and feeling her way, tripped on a science book. She lay in bed in the blackness of the room. 'I can't believe it, I'll have to look up sleepwalking behaviours tomorrow. That was unbelievable she looked straight at me. Over-excitement. Why the hell did that meteor spin us all out? Christ, I better not tell Mum or she'll be off like a lunatic.' She tossed and felt for her blankets to shrug off the cold.

At six-fifteen, the usual alarm didn't go off. Instead, Amy was awoken by her mother, who beamed down like some beneficent Jesus.

'Amy, Amy,' she whispered in tones nearly too low to disturb a dream. 'Evie can see, Evie can see.'

And the two women in their blazing white nighties smiled over Amy's bed.

Amy shook. 'What's going on?' she asked crankily.

'Eve can see. Look at her. She can see again. Go on, Eve. What colour is Amy wearing?'

'She's got a blue and yellow top on with black dogs on it.'

Amy, not even aware of what she was wearing, looked down at her nightie. 'Did you tell her?' she said to her mother.

'Why would I tell her? She can SEE.'

She noticed her father quietly appear at the door with a quizzical look. From the smell, he had been out the back smoking and contemplating.

'Come on, ask her what colour anything is.'

'She's not a performing animal, Mum. Can I ask her if she thinks you've aged since she could see you last?'

'Oh, Amy.' Her mother laughed it off. 'Come on, Eve, it's a day for celebration. I'll ring the rest of the family.'

The two of them flew out of the room as though swept up by wings. Only Paul remained.

'What's happening, Dad?'

'I dunno. But she genuinely can see. Try to be happy for her, Ames.'

'I am. Truly. But it just doesn't make sense. She came in during the night. I thought it was a dream. I don't understand. She needs to get to her doctor and find out what it's all about. I'm afraid for them.'

'Don't be afraid. Be happy. They'll cope, whatever happens. Your mum thinks it was what happened last night.'

'Yeah, but we know it wasn't that. Don't turn batty like her, Dad. You know what she's like. One religious zealot in the family is enough.'

'I know, Ames, but it makes you wonder.'

'Yeah. It does. I'll see what I can find out over at the medical department today.'

Amy returned home early from university as she had promised her mother. It was a compromise because she hadn't stayed home for the miraculous event. She turned the corner and noticed a mobile film crew outside the house. 'Shit.' As she neared the tired brick veneer, she noticed the front door open and strangers passing cables and equipment through. 'What the hell?' she said more to herself than the two men busy hoisting lights.

'Amy, Amy, quickly. Come inside. We've just had an interview with Ranald Rollings.'

'But you hate his show. You're always saying it's about boob jobs and diets.'

'Shhhh,' Marie hissed and glared at Amy as they passed the film crew. 'We're going to be on TV. Oh, it's such a day,' she said and ushered Amy through the lounge room that had been re-arranged spectacularly to accommodate the television crew.

She noticed Dad's moss green easy chair had been moved out of the room to make way for a seat that she hadn't seen before. The shabby sofa had been transformed by the clever use of a new off-white throw rug. At the rear of that a white screen had been arranged to hide the doors that led to the darkened hall. Marie's hideously ugly Italian Virgin figurine stood on a pedestal table in front of the screen. And amid the bustle Eve sat benignly watching a Raphael-like pale cherub with impassive eyes. The translucence of her skin reflected the absurdly bright lights that had not yet been dismantled and were still on, making everyone sweat.

Marie's sisters Kathy and Laura fluffed about in the kitchen, while their children, bored by lack of attention, entertained themselves by stuffing huge hunks of Black Forest cake into their mouths and flicking potato chips at one another. Marie's best friend Chris and her two young children were knocking themselves over to be noticed. And Father Flanagan, who Marie had known since school, sat on the vinyl kitchen chair, sipping a steaming tea, looking awkwardly towards the men who were downing VBs outside in a mist of smoke.

Amy pulled a beer out of the fridge and, handing it to Father Flanagan, set a chair down beside him.

'Listen, this is all bullshit, isn't it?' she said accusingly.

'Oh, hello, Amy. I'm good, thanks. What about you?'

'Yeah, yeah. Hello, Michael. How are you?' she asked in a mocking tone. 'So did the stupid fart ask you anything?'

'I take it you mean the erudite Mr Rollings? And thanks for the beer by the way,' he said as a sigh emerged from both him and the can.

'Yeah.'

'Nothing.'

'Nothing?'

'Well, nothing that will be aired on his enlightening show.'

'Whadya mean?'

'He asked me if I would be happy to be interviewed about it, which I agreed to, and then he asked me if I thought it was a miracle, and after I gave him my answer he just ignored me.'

'What did you say?'

'Well, what can you say, Amy? I can't give him his miracle. Anyway, what I said wasn't what he wanted so he just up and walked away. Charming bloke.'

'Everyone will be wanting a miracle and you're the so-called expert. You could have picked up a few more parishioners with bait like that and got 'em hook, line and sinker.'

'Is that how you get 'em, Amy? Is that how I'd get you? A definite answer? A supposed miracle?' Michael Flanagan smiled at her as he pressed the cold tin in his hands and felt it buckle slightly. 'No, Amy. A miracle to me is when people believe even when they've been given no definite answer.'

'You're hoping for too much.'

'I'm always hopeful.'

It was three days before the interview screened on the *Newsworthy* program with the tag *Daily news worthy of more investigation*. The family gathered around the television, listening to the theme music as they sat on the newly arranged seats. Paul sat uncomfortably on the new chair. Marie's eyes glistened, Eve sat placidly watching everything and Amy sat on the floor picking dirt off the carpet.

'Tonight we have a special story about a girl who regained her sight overnight – the church claims it could be a miracle…'

'Well, that's bullsh. Michael didn't say that. That's for sure.'

'Shoosh, Amy. Maybe someone else did,' Mum whispered

'I think the operative word is "could",' Paul advised.

They watched as their reality was conveyed back to them on a box – their colours and images dispersed from the eye of a lens and re-emerging with sound waves through a cathode tube onto a screen made of minuscule dots – a kind of reality.

On the screen, Marie and Paul nestled tightly on either side of Eve. A room that they knew to be theirs came screaming back at them with a dazzling white, draped background and sofa cover. The story neatly commencing the morning after the 'miracle' when Evie told her mother that she could see, thereby absolving Amy from a duty to be there and face dangerous questioning. Marie was overjoyed, Paul thought it was fantastic and Evie could not be prompted to say more than, 'It's really good to see.'

The segment fitted in nicely before an advertisement for a product to get rid of blackheads. But not before the viewers were invited to enter a *Newsworthy* poll conducted on the question of 'Do you believe that Eve Somerton regained her sight because of a miracle? Here are the numbers on the screen. Remember to SMS or phone before midnight tonight and you could be in the lucky draw for a holiday for two to Green Island.'

The family sat in silence for some seconds.

'Let's vote, Mum,' Amy chirruped in a way that birds do just before sunset.

'Geez, it didn't look like our house, did it?' said Paul, shocked.

'Eve, you looked beautiful,' Marie cried.

'Mum, you looked so happy,' Eve murmured plaintively.

'Mum, you looked like your head was going to explode,' Amy choked out.

'I can't believe they would do that,' Paul said as he got up from the seat and went to sit on the back step holding a chilled ale close to him.

Three days after the family appeared on *Newsworthy*, Amy walked into Eve's room and found her with her head in her hands. 'How's it going, Eyes? What's wrong?'

'My head is aching, Amy.'

'Well, you keep looking into that computer screen and you're not used to it. Give it a rest for a while.'

'No. It's not that.' Eve sat quietly for a moment. 'My eyes…I can't see so well…things are getting blurry…'

'We have to get you to a doctor. Now,' Amy demanded.

'Amy, it's all right. I can deal with it,' she smiled and took Amy's hand.

Amy withdrew it suddenly. 'No. No. No. Shit, shit, shit.'

There was nothing they could do, the specialists said. The medical department at uni had no answers either.

By the third week, Eve could only see bright lights. 'I'm glad the circus is over, Ame. It was wonderful to see again, it was like a looking through a window and seeing the world in its brilliance, but it looked black too.'

'It was a bit shit, is what it was. I'm researching it. I won't let it go.'

'You're a funny old thing, Amy. You wouldn't accept that I could see and now you won't accept that I can't.'

'The only good thing to come out of it was that the eighty-six per cent of ignoramuses who said it was a miracle on that current affair show were wrong,' Amy spat with contempt.

'You are so mean. Did you really watch to see what the figure was?' Evie said shocked. 'Geez, I didn't think you of all people would be taken in by a stupid poll hook, line and sinker.'

Amy felt the crush of the words. She needed to speak to make sure her voice could be heard. 'Mum would have been happy with the result,' her voice crackling.

'Mum was appalled.'

Amy looked up and said with a voice quieter than a leaf falling. 'How is Mum? I'm too afraid to talk to her about it.'

'She's good…disappointed, knocked around, but she only cares about me. Not the rest of it.'

'So she's not destroyed?'

'No. Never destroyed. Always hopeful.'

The television was on in the lounge room. Paul sat on his green chair, which had re-appeared. He read the newspaper taken from a stack behind the sofa. The throw rug sat in a crumpled heap next to the papers where it had slid off. Marie came in with a cup of tea and placed it on the pedestal table knocking the ugly Virgin figurine. The theme music for *Newsworthy* started to play.

'We're not watching that wanker,' Paul asserted.

Amy sat by the window in her room punching numbers into her calculator and looked up for a moment to watch the stars. She noticed some nimbus stratus clouds veil parts of the sky. She noticed the stars reappear from the mist when it floated away. She knew they were light years away. A swirling, dynamic galaxy. But they were sparkling and clear and gorgeous. She had never seen them that way before.

The Pinnacle

The air is crisp with clarity first thing in the morning at The Pinnacle. The sea resembles cream leather where the sun is rising and close by the gulls fight like urchins and churn the air. To the south of The Pinnacle lookout, Chapel Beach is being pummelled by pearly surf.

It isn't long before two surfies climb the path and join me with a nod and a 'Hey' to survey the shifty ocean in search of swell. They wait for the beat of the sea to reveal itself if it wants to. They linger, shifting their thonged feet in the grainy dirt while their arms rest uneasily on the weathered fence. Their eyes are willing goliath obsidian scrolls of water but there is only slopping currents of trickery. They keep shifting their feet and straining their eyes against the determined rays of sunlight. The gulls burn up in the golden light and slide into the coolness below.

The surfies don't say a word for quite a while as they watch through guarded eyes.

At last the one with the faded green windcheater claims, 'There's nothin.' He shields his eyes hurt by the glare creeping in at the side. He stands straight and tall. He has made his decision.

The breeze picks up a curly strand of bleached hair and gently blows it away from his face so that he may get a clearer view. I glance across and recognise something in him. A dryness needing the salve of water. I know that look.

His mate, more stocky, stretches and opens the cracks of parched skin. The sunlight reflects a curious darkness from his smooth brown hair. 'Yeeaaaoh,' he dreamily croons and curls his body back into a hunch on the rail. 'I need breakfast, man. This is crap.'

They trundle the well-worn path back down to the car park and I know in an hour they will be out there clinging to their boards.

Above the restless gnashing of waves I hear the call of 'Hello, Mum,' as my daughter spots me from the beach, her hair electrified in a wild golden storm of protest and face spotty and fair, looking so familiar. I lean to the rail and wave and as I replace my hand, see the outline of a shape carved long ago. The blistered shards of white paint surrounding bare timber lines make it nearly unrecognisable as a heart shape.

It is a particular smell that of tea tree and salt. The way the air starts to waft up after sunrise is characteristic of this point. It's a while since I have been here to watch the sun rise and let it drift over me like I used to with Michael. It would wrap around us with the tenderness of a hug until the breeze sharpened us awake. We would run back down the track and nick our bare toes on roots and stones, unhook the boards from the EH wagon and run to the beach as though it would not last.

Never as game as Michael, I would follow him into the water as the sea would rise and block him out of my view and then fall in a diastolic hollow. We would ride the turbid rip out and be surrendered to the forming waves out the back. He would always get the first wave and I would be left there fearful and alone in the grip of an ocean until he returned. He would encourage me to climb a gentle wave. 'That's it. Go, girl,' as I struggled into a standing position in momentary victory. I would then fall ungraciously into the water. For me it was all about being with him in this place. I was no surfer and the cold and my inability would force me out onto the beach to grill in between bikini lines, while he continued to tunnel through walls of water.

Michael would be out there for hours and when he had grown too tired to surf we would visit The Greek Temple at the local shops for one flake to share and two or three potato cakes, depending on how much money we could scrounge. We would sit at the red laminated tables opposite one another and unwrap the steaming food and hoe in. I would look across at him. He was like some god to me. His curly hair would catch the light in glistening platinum arcs. His shining face, with summer freckles joining together triumphantly across it, would crease into laughter at stupid things.

One time we made the mistake of bringing our two best friends Steve and Amanda. They complained about driving for an hour so early in the morning to get here in a car, which had a window that wouldn't shut and made the trip a turbulent and cold event. When we arrived at the lookout they puffed so hard that they couldn't see the vastness. After an hour on the beach, Amanda decided to walk up the main street to look for clothes in the few tourist shops that existed then and Steve sat in Michael's car sweating and listening to the one-day cricket match at the MCG. Michael and I looked at one another. No one else was ever invited again.

Just before one Christmas, a huge storm hit. The air had been close, bugged with flies and sticky. The sun had risen and we said that it looked like bloody shipwrecks of clouds in the eastern sky. As we watched from the lookout, an old local called Joey with dreadlocked hair warned in a bass voice, 'Red sky in the morning...' He didn't finish the saying and walked off back down the track. Michael and I looked at one another, used to stoned locals.

'What was he on about?' he whispered into my ear.

Thrilled by his breath, I whispered back, 'I dunno.' But I did and took no heed.

At about eleven o'clock a coolness charged the air. Great cumulonimbus clouds started to bunch along the horizon until they darkened to pitch. The waves became haphazard. I was on the beach as the wind blew. Michael of course couldn't resist the terror of the ride and refused to come out. As the seas slapped and spouted, my view of him was interrupted. The wind raced and swept sand into a stinging veil. Dazzling shafts of lighting speared the sea. Michael needed to get out. I started shouting amid the deafening winds, but my voice shot backwards. The sand continued blasting my face and grit lodged in my eyes blocking my vision. Tears formed and all I could see was opaque and senseless. I wailed for Michael and cried.

The sky blackened and large drops of rain started to fall. Then, as if to take a breath, the wind died and the rain abated. In that moment I thought it would stop. But it poured down again with reinforced strength. I continued blindly shouting in the drenching rain.

A thick yellow towel was slung over my head. 'Fran, you idiot, what are you doing? Come on, let's go.'

We sat shivering on the vinyl benchseats of his Holden, our combined breath fogging up the interior windows while torrents of rain poured down. We watched the ragged clouds and the climbing sea fragmenting through the arching tea tree. The wind battered the car and shook it. The lightning whipped the sky. The path to the lookout became a brown river of sand and dirt making a slurry that spread across the car park to the drains that gagged from the overflow.

Michael relished it and I, being naturally afraid, was carried along with his courage.

'Did you think I wouldn't come out?' he laughed.

'I knew you wouldn't come out,' I said with mock irritation. 'Thank heavens that old guy made you.'

He chuckled. 'You know me better than anyone.'

We sat ensconced in a cocoon of wet towels as he wrapped his arms around my purpling skin and watched the craziness swirl around us as the water in the car park rose alarmingly. Some of the shops got flooded. The fish and chip shop got struck by lightning. It closed down after that. We were devastated.

A gull lands unsteadily on the rail and eyes me with hope.

'Mum, come down,' Shania urges from the beach.

The bright yellow sun is rolling into the sky and the familiar rush of air peels across the furrows of my forehead. I rest a little longer after the trudge to the lookout and seek to relieve the pressure of weight upon my legs. My stance changes but there is still an ache. I glance again at the carving. One name is nearly worn away, the other totally.

I watch Shania on the beach. She starts to run across the shallows. The ridges look like postmarks on an aged letter from another time.

She looks back at me and waves. She tells me that she wants to try surfing. She says, 'I'll be careful, Mum.'

I always say no.

Love All

'Nadal needs to come into the net, mix it up a bit. He's too far behind the baseline.'

The television commentators agreed and Geoff felt vindicated. His could feel a twinge in his elbow as his weathered arm reached for the chilled ginger ale which sat on the coffee table along with greasy dinner plates. He felt the slippery dampness of the glass. The ice clinked gently as he brought it to his lips. He sipped the contents and licked his lips after swallowing the bubbling drink. It cooled him, as did the regular puff of air from the oscillating fan as it blew past him and then across to the other side of the room where Edie sat.

'Would you like another one, love?' he asked her out of habit.

She smiled at him but didn't answer. It was a warm night and had been a hot day, so he poured another half a glass for her. She used to love a ginger ale.

'This is a good game,' he told her. 'It'll probably go all night.' He took a handful of peanuts from the bowl and offered her some.

She took them and nibbled as though out of duty not indulgence.

'Sho-ot,' he sang. 'They're nearly as good as we used to be, Eed. But not as much style, eh?' he smiled 'Your forehand was copybook. And your backhand was pretty good too – lovely follow through. None of this double-handed stuff,' he said dismissively.

'Yes. Yes, it was,' she answered dreamy-eyed. 'I played tennis,' she told him suddenly. 'I won the club championship. I beat Gracie O'Leary.'

'Yes, dear. I remember.'

'Were you there?'

'Yes, dear, I was there.'

He picked up the plates when the set was finished. 'I'll just do these dishes. Why don't you get ready for bed, or do you want to stay up and watch more of the game?' he asked stupidly, knowing that the decision would be his.

She looked at him as though waiting for directions.

'It might get a bit late for you. You hop off to bed. I'll just give these dishes a wash and then I'll come in to say goodnight. OK, love?'

'Yes, yes,' she said obligingly and toddled off towards the bathroom.

Geoff slapped the dishes and cutlery in and out of the soapy water in the sink and left them foaming in the rack. A quick kiss and a tuck-in and he would be back in the lounge room for the remaining sets.

He congratulated himself on his tennis knowledge. Watching the game brought back memories of conquests he had on and off the court at his old club Surrey Pines. They used to skylark, the boys Sam, Lochie and Oscar, who were in his team. They took on all-comers, beating most, winning championships with such regularity that they were called The Masters. They strutted, flexed their muscles, limbered up like gazelles, especially in front of the girls.

Then one day, a memorable day, a girl with high cheeks, sleepy blue eyes and long wavy hair came to the club. Edwina Swinton. The boys made a beeline for her – a stylish bit of new blood whose lithe physique moved elegantly under her tantalising tennis dress, and she had a game to match. They cavorted and fooled in front of her. Hit brash shots, slid dangerously for backhands and pounced recklessly for dribbling volleys. But she always flicked her ponytail, lowered her eyes and sauntered off. They decided that she was a snob and stuck up, while each of them secretly harboured a desire to take her on their arm.

Geoff, though, happened to run into her often after matches and practice, quietly inquiring about the outcome of her games. Sometimes they had a hit and she smashed a few past him as he wilted willingly. Geoff half smiled.

The empty drink cans were tossed into the bin and the table hastily

wiped as Geoff held the cloth to his chest, took a peremptory look over
the kitchen ascertaining that it was good enough. He stole a chocolate
from the fridge and one for Edie. He threw it in his mouth, walked
though the lounge room to the drone of John McEnroe and glanced
at the score. 'Yes, he's come back.' One set all. He looked at the silent
clock on the wall as it flicked away the seconds. He was prepared to
settle in for a late game after saying goodnight.

As he passed the hall table, his eye, accustomed now to domestic
aesthetics, noticed the framed photo of Edie hugging their two boys
a little askew. He picked up the photo and realigned the stand, taking
a moment. It was taken on a holiday to Queensland when John was
ten and Grant twelve. They had all been on some wild ride that turned
them upside down and their hair was standing on end. It was a crazy
photo and they looked a mess but the normally graceful Edie insisted
on it being displayed. It was the first time that they had been north. It
had been the best time.

He walked to the bedroom, where a soft lamp lit the dusky pink
room. As he did, he noticed the latch on the fly wire door had opened
and he snibbed the lock before entering the bedroom. He expected
Edie to be tucked up with her eyes wandering, watching, waiting. The
bed was still made. Untouched. Geoff doubled back to the bathroom,
where the light blazed, so he went back to the lounge room and stood
watching the tennis, waiting for Edie to finish in there.

The tennis was transfixing. The players powerful. Playing shots
with such force that the reaction of the other was only reflex. Such
warriors. Such gladiators. After several minutes, Geoff glanced back up
the passage to see the light still shining from the bathroom.

'Are you OK, dear?' he asked dutifully.

There was no answer.

The sweat dripped from the players' faces. They called for towels
before each serve. It must have still been in the high thirties on centre
court. The fan blew the stuffy air around the room. He could feel the
feebleness of it at the boundary of its powers where he stood.

'Love?' he called. Again there was no answer. Not that he expected one.

He walked up to the bathroom. Edie was not in there. Nor was she in the toilet. She must be in bed now, he thought, as he replayed Nadal's last shot in his mind. The power – how would you return a shot like that? You would return it without thinking, with a shot that you had played thousands, maybe hundreds of thousands of times before. A shot you had practised over and over because you loved the game.

He entered the bedroom again. The bed was made. No figure curled in readiness for sleep, no head resting upon the pillow with child-like expectation. 'Edie? Edie? Where are you, love?' he called flatly.

Checking the toilet and the bathroom again, Geoff decided to search the other rooms as he had done on other occasions, turning the lights on as he did so. He looked in the spare bedroom, where the sewing machine sat cobwebby on the table next to faded fabric. He moved to the front lounge room calling, 'Edie. Edie, love.' He went into the backyard, flicking the switch and flooding a stark light on the paved courtyard. It cast shadows across two empty teacups that sat on the garden table from the morning, the dregs of which had dried and contracted into two pronounced rings.

Hearing a reassuring click from inside, he entered again and on his way through the house he paused to watch Nadal swipe at a passing winner. He headed up the hall to the bedroom. Locked in a kind of groundhog day scenario, he again saw the bed undisturbed. He wandered about the house calling for Edie and inspected rooms again.

'God damn,' he whispered. 'Edie,' he called with more breath. 'Come on, my dear, off to bed now,' as though she would respond. But she didn't. And he sighed and clicked his tongue.

In the hall he stood with his hands on his hips. His brows rough. His eyes strained. He gazed up the hall to the bedroom with the soft illumination glowing from within. A moth thumped against the fly wire door catching his attention. 'Shit.'

Lurching into the middle of the street, he peered up and down.

'Edie,' he called each way before deciding to follow the road to the busier end of the street where it intersected with the main road out of the estate. 'Christ, come on, old girl,' he said to himself as he paced up the road.

Two women were walking their dog and appeared guarded as he approached them from the middle of the road.

'Have you seen an elderly lady walking up the road.'

'No,' they said, 'but we'll keep a look out.'

'Her name is Edwina – Edie.'

'OK,' they said uncertainly. 'What number are you if we see her.'

'Twenty-one.'

'OK.' They drifted into the darkness, their assurances as unknown as the tightly packed night.

She couldn't have gone far. Surely.

The giddy moths circled the creamy street light, battering against it in endless attraction. It threw mottled grey patches between eucalypt saplings that stirred to rising air pressure. He searched with his eyes for any movement up and down the street. He noticed some, metres away, but realised that it was the women he had spoken to moments before crossing the nature strip to the road.

As he circled the block, forms appeared only to be gone again as he neared. His senses sharpened and he became jittery. The former champion pulled on reserves of strength. But he was no longer young. Pacing quickly along the road, he could feel his heart thump terribly against his chest. His temples throbbed. His calves no longer sprang against resistance. His shoulders and neck were stiff and unyielding. He started to doubt. He started to feel weak.

He turned for home and raced to get his car keys. Was it too early to ring the police? The front light was switched on and he left the door open. In his car he could search more streets and the light would be constant. But he would be prevented from entering other darker places.

Ahead there was a boy on his bike – too bloody young to be out this late. A couple jogging. A family with ice creams. An old man with a supermarket bag. Another couple with a pram and a dog. Lights flashed from other cars. In the distance, engines revved, brakes screeched and youths surrendered time and energy to elevate their manhood. He felt vulnerable. Edie was vulnerable.

He needed help. At home he would phone the police. He would alert the neighbours. He would phone John and Grant. His eyes darted along the road to the house. All was quiet. He turned into the driveway and saw figures at the front door with the light blazing like the annunciation.

Edie was serenely staring from within the house, her soft eyes roaming behind the wire door.

The two women and their dog were glowing under the light. 'We went searching the streets and asked some people. We came back to see if you needed help to find her and she was just up at that house over there,' they said, pointing.

Geoff could hardly speak, as though he had swallowed string. He kissed them both. Then the two women and their dog were gathered into the night and he entered the house after locking both doors behind him. Behind the doors he sobbed and although she had no idea why he took her hand and gently kissed it this night she gave a little smile.

He closed the bedroom door behind him and checked the entrance again. He turned off the lights. One by one. He lingered in the hall. His elbow ached as he raised it to the switch. He entered the kitchen and silently put the dried dishes and cutlery away, filled the last glass with water from the tap and bowed his head exhaustedly. He took the drink into the lounge room and collapsed into the lounge chair. The television was still on and Nadal and his opponent were two sets each. He sat to watch the last set. He wondered how long it would last.

Planned Obsolescence

Gina tried to attach a document to her email. She barely heard the train pounding the tracks outside her window. Again she searched for the file. Hit. Enter. Nothing. Heavy dusty curtains raggedly framed the railway wires swinging in the wake of the six-fifteen from the city. Enter. Nothing. Stringy frustration writhed in her guts. Enter. Enter. Enter. She looked through the scratchy window and noticed how the niggardly wires always stopped a clear view of the sky.

'That computer is too old. Get rid of it. Get a new one. They're not supposed to last forever,' Jason her son complained from the threadbare maroon couch.

'I'm not made of money to be buying computers on a whim,' she droned on.

Her bee-like noise could make you sleepy. It deserved to be swiped. He opened a packet of potato chips and crammed a handful into his mouth. Chewing shut her out. He turned on the TV to be sure.

'Can you turn that TV down?' she buzzed.

'What?'

'TURN THE TV DOWN,' whined the bee.

'ALL RIGHT.'

'I'M TRYING TO WORK.'

'I'M TRYING TO WATCH TV.'

'YOU SHOULD BE DOING YOUR HOMEWORK.'

'YOU SHOULD BE COOKING MY TEA.'

High-pitched squealing, like insects ready to strike.

Windows trembled from the grind of the passing city trains. Gina took her work into her bedroom. Layers of clothes toppled from her bed, papers piled upon the heaving dresser. After shuffling some messy manila files off her desk, she turned the computer on and successfully sent the email and document. She breathed shallow little ping-pong ball breaths. Stupid ineffectual breaths, that sucked in tension. Try to calm down before you go out to the kitchen. Make him wait. He can't tell you to make his tea like that. Make him wait. Soulless little shit.

Her eyes searched the room for something solid, something comforting. They rested on a framed photo of a beaming woman and a small baby in swaddling clothes. She sat back on the timber chair and heard it creak, ready to snap. At last the breaths came back in big balloon shapes. The computer screen went blank and she wondered what the hell was in the pantry.

The fridge door squeaked opened with a sigh. Lettuce, tomato… carrot. Chicken.

The inevitable 'What are we having for tea?' spat through mouthfuls of masticated mush.

'Chicken.'

'Chicken? I had chicken at Dad's last night.'

'Do you want chicken or nothing?'

'Why can't we have some meat?'

'Because we ate the meat the night before.'

'Haven't we got anything else?'

'No, we haven't got anything else.'

'I'll have baked beans on toast.'

'BUT I'VE STARTED COOKING THE CHICKEN.'

'FORGET IT. I'LL PUT ON BAKED BEANS.'

'ALL RIGHT, I WILL FORGET IT.'

'Are you going to put them on?'

'I'll do it later.'

'Do you want me to put them on?'

'NO, I'LL DO IT LATER, I SAID.'

'FINE. MAKE SURE YOU DO.' Drone. Drone. Drone.

He continued stuffing potato chips. The TV was so loud no one knew what they were saying.

Gina sat at the back step. Her bum rested awkwardly on the hard bricks. She opened a stubby, hearing the release of pressure, and regretted it immediately. She poured the liquid into the glass, chilling her hand. I'm sick of this, she thought. She gazed past the patchy timber fence to the frail slice of moon baking on half-lit lemon light, a backdrop to the silhouettes of half-full suburban trains that trundled and trundled.

Loud spaces in conversation upset her so much these days that the frying chicken strips almost set her at ease. From the back step she could hear it sizzle and smell the familiar, but it was starting to burn. Tiredly she stood to enter the house and knocked over the stubby. There were almost tears in her eyes. I didn't want that anyway, she thought, as the glass jangled. She watched the fluid froth and flow down the steps and onto a patch of dirt. She brought the chipped plate out onto the step and sat picking at the drowning lettuce and tomato.

The boy had taken her most tender piece of chicken out of the pan with his greasy hand and eaten it right in front of her. 'Why didn't you make some for me?' he winked.

A minute later she was at the back fence and lifting her leg up to the second rail. She could hear the trickety track a long way before she could even see the light. And the wirey vibrations. If she put her head on the rails, she would even be able to feel it. The solid coldness. She could tell the future.

She kicked the ballast as she walked up the line and almost tripped on the sleepers in her flapping thongs.

Above, the sleepy stars started to wake and assemble at the darker edges of sky. The insects began their nocturnal rounds with zeal.

'Mum, we've got no bread.' He chomped at the blue screen. 'We've got no bread. WE'VE GOT NO BREAD.'

Then it went silent.

Gina scrambled down the other side of the tracks and over a fence. Curling the rubber thong and feeling incredibly old and weathered.

'Starlight, star bright, first star out tonight,' she said to herself. She spent a second to reattach the thong, putting down the five dollars in loose change on the footpath.

www.ingramcontent.com/pod-product-compliance
Lightning Source LLC
Chambersburg PA
CBHW020347110726
47898CB00003B/1081